VEDAVALLI AND THE PRINCE

A HISTORICAL TALE OF BETRAYAL, AND REVENGE AND LOVE

DIVYASSHREE

To the beauty of the past, which can still teach us so much about ourselves.

Contents

Contents

Prologue

In a realm of shifting alliances and turbulent times, where power and destiny intertwine, the King of Anga, Ramachandra emerged triumphant, quashing revolts that threatened his rule not only within the boundaries of Anga itself but also among its minor kingdoms. Yet, as fate would have it, even in the face of victory, tragedy struck the King's life. He and his beloved wife, Padma, a pillar of strength and grace, met an untimely end in a hunting accident. Little opposition ensued when his brother Vikrama took over the crown soon after. King Vikrama was a member of the council known for his lobbying skills, many did not see him as a leader.

Adjoining Anga was the land of Malla, ruled by one of the most powerful crowned queens in the world. Queen Mahadevi was a wise and just ruler, but she was also a very private person. She rarely confided in anyone, except for Vedavalli, whom she had trained personally. Vedavalli came alone to the palace as a young girl, hoping to find a place in the queen's service. The queen saw in Vedavalli a burning desire to rise, a determination to prove herself, and all of this and more.

Years have gone and Vedavalli still stood behind the Queen, supporting her reign. And for the first time, she is about to go against the throne.

CHAPTER ONE

Vedavalli sat at her desk, surrounded by piles of notes. She was in the middle of preparing for the daily durbar, a meeting held between the queen, and her advisors. The council was the highest advisory body in the kingdom. She had just finished drafting a proposal to increase the number of elephant troops stationed at the border when a messenger knocked urgently at her door.

She put down her stylus and opened the door to find a young man, out of breath and covered in dust. He handed her a thick letter with the nail barely holding the palm leaves together, bearing the seal of Anga. Vedavalli's heart sank as she read it.

As the nephew to the current King, Prince Mukund was known to voice his concerns about his uncle's decisions. Even Vedavalli had heard of his skills as a strategist. Having met him only once when his father was alive and ruling, she believed that if he was accused of a crime things might be serious in Anga.

Vedavalli had to make a decision. If she helped Mukund, it would likely mean more problems for Malla.

Elsewhere, Prince Mukund's heart raced as he sprinted through the unfamiliar terrain, his eyes scanning the horizon for any sign of the Malla kingdom. He was bruised and battered, his clothes torn and dirty.

The sound of hooves grew louder behind him, telling him that the soldiers were getting closer. He pushed himself even harder, his feet pounding the dirt as he ran. The trees rushed by him in a blur, and he could feel the sweat pouring down his face.

He remembered his uncle's last words before he escaped.

"You have brought shame upon our family and our kingdom, Mukund," his uncle spat out in disgust. "I cannot allow you to take the throne."

Mukund felt a wave of anger and frustration wash over him. He had never wanted to cause any harm to his family or his kingdom, but circumstances had forced his hand.

"I did not want this, Uncle," Mukund pleaded, his eyes locked on his uncle's. "I only wanted what was best for our people, for Anga!" He shook himself free of the guards' clasp who found themselves in an unwanted family spat.

"You do not get to decide what is best for our people, boy," his uncle retorted. "You are not fit to rule, and you will never sit on the throne."

Mukund felt a lump form in his throat as he realized the finality of his uncle's words. He knew he had to flee; he could not be captured and subjected to his uncle's wrath. Without a word, he turned and began to walk towards the door. But before he could take more than a few steps, he felt a strong grip on his arm.

"You think you can just walk away from this?" his uncle hissed, his face twisted in rage. "You will pay for what you have done."

With a sudden burst of strength, he wrenched his arm free from his uncle's grasp and broke into a run towards the door. The guards tried to grab him, but Mukund was faster.

He dashed out of the room and into the palace courtyard, his heart pounding in his chest. He kept running without looking back. He didn't know how he was going to make it to the border, but he had to keep going. Even as his legs grew tired and his breaths came in gasps.

On hearing the news, Vedavalli's first thought was to bring this to the queen's attention. But, before she could even react, another messenger came with the news that Prince Mukund had crossed the border albeit full of injuries.

Fate had finally placed a key in her hand. A key she will use to lock the murderer of her past in the prison cell.

As she sat alone in her chamber, Vedavalli wondered if she should help the Prince. However, as soon as she presented her stance to the queen and the other advisors, Ojayjit, the chief strategist, opposed her plan vehemently, claiming that it would put the kingdom in danger and that giving asylum to the prince would be a mistake. Ojayjit's arguments were persuasive. He pointed out that giving asylum to the Prince would be a clear signal to Anga that Malla was unwilling to negotiate the ownership of Kshatriyapuram. This could make Anga more likely to go to war, and it could also put Malla at a disadvantage in any future negotiations.

As soon as the meeting was over, Vedavalli made her way to the queen's chambers. She knocked on the door and, without waiting for an answer, barged in.

"Your Majesty, I cannot in good conscience escort Prince Mukund back to Anga. He is innocent and would face certain death if he were returned."

Also, he is the answer to my prayers, she thought. All along, while rising to power Vedavalli waited for a chance to receive closure to her past. Now that closure arrived in the form of Prince Mukund. But no one can know about it. So she kept her thoughts to herself.

The queen looked up at Vedavalli with a hard expression. "Vedavalli, you know that the kingdom's alliance with Anga is of the utmost importance. We cannot risk that even for the prince. The new king..." her voice trailed.

The previous's King and Queen's sudden demise affected Malla. The two Queens Mahadevi and Padma were best friends.

"I understand that, Your Majesty, but we cannot simply throw an innocent man to the wolves. He has been falsely accused and we have an obligation to protect him."

The queen looked at Vedavalli for a moment, then let out a sigh. "Very well. Prince Mukund may stay in the palace guest lodgings until we can figure out a way to clear his name."

Vedavalli breathed a sigh of relief. "Thank you, Your Majesty. I will see to it that he is taken care of."

And with that, Vedavalli left the queen's chambers, her mind racing with possibilities of how to prove Prince Mukund's innocence.

CHAPTER TWO

Queen Mahadevi stood on the balcony, staring at the moon as if asking it for answers. The Queen furrowed her brow.

"Where is Vedavalli?" she asked, referring to her trusted advisor.

"She has gone to prepare the guest lodgings," Ojayjit replied.

Queen Mahadevi chuckled. "Thought so."

The Queen looked thoughtful for a moment before turning to Ojayjit and asking, "I don't know, Minister. But I have a feeling that Vedavalli is more invested in finding the culprit than she is letting on. Do you think there's another motive?"

Ojayjit's eyes narrowed at the mention of Vedavalli's name. He knew that she was a threat to his power and influence in the palace. "It's hard to say, Your Majesty," he replied, his voice tight. "Vedavalli has always been dedicated to serving the kingdom and protecting its people. But perhaps there is something else at play here."

The Queen nodded thoughtfully. "Vedavalli's family moved in from Anga during the farmers' uprising. There are few accounts of a younger sibling that passed away young. I did not dig into it, out of respect for her wishes to bury those memories. But I have a feeling that there is more to the story. Can you look into that?"

Ojayjit felt a jolt of fear and excitement run through him at the Queen's request. He knew that Vedavalli's past was a tangled web of secrets and lies, and he relished the opportunity to uncover them. "Me?" he mumbled before nodding vigorously, "It is an honor, Your Majesty."

Ten years ago, when Ojayjit was 16 years old, he joined the Malla army. He quickly rose through the ranks, and he soon became a respected captain. But his rise to power was not without its challenges. He had made many enemies along the way, and he knew that they would not hesitate to see him dead if they had the chance.

But Ojayjit was not afraid. He was a survivor, and he would do whatever it took to protect his power and influence. Even if it meant digging up Vedavalli's past.

Vedavalli was busy making arrangements for Prince Mukund's stay in the palace guest lodgings. She needed him on her side to tell the world of all the deeds King Vikrama had done. Mukund had once gone against his uncle, which prepared him for an incoming war. The war would be between power and truth, and it was unknown which side Mukund would stand with.

As she was making her rounds, she received a message from the palace guard that Prince Mukund had been injured while on the run. She immediately rushed to the palace infirmary, where she found the prince lying on a bed, his arm bandaged and his face pale.

"What happened?" Vedavalli asked the palace physician.

"He was injured in a fight with some of the soldiers. He's lucky to be alive," the physician replied.

Vedavalli's heart sank as she looked at the prince's injuries. She stayed by his side, holding his hand and talking to him softly until he fell asleep. Kindness and compassion were the best healers, and she extended this to all of her closest companions, regardless of their gender. Like her, life had been cruel to Prince Mukund as well, taking his family away from him too soon.

As she was leaving the infirmary, she ran into Ojayjit. The chief strategist looked at her with a mixture of concern and curiosity. "How is he?" Ojayjit asked.

Vedavalli looked at him with suspicion, wondering why he was showing concern for the prince. "He's injured, but he'll be okay," she replied.

Ojayjit nodded and said, "If there's anything I can do to help, please let me know." Vedavalli was surprised by Ojayjit's offer, but she didn't say anything.

That night as she sat alone in her room looking at the sculptures carved in the pillars, the lamp in the room dimmed and the shadows on her face deepened.

Suddenly, there was a knock on the door. She quickly composed herself. She called out, "Come in."

The door opened, and Ojayjit entered. As he held a lamp, the light shone directly on his face, creating a contrast with Vedavalli's shadows.

Vedavalli was growing increasingly suspicious about Ojayjit's intentions and his offer to help Prince Mukund. He had betrayed her before for wealth. She couldn't trust him once again with a secret.

Also, her spy came back to her with a report that there was a girl who had recently arrived in the capital and that she seemed to be searching for someone from Anga. Vedavalli immediately ordered her spy to trail the girl and find out who she was and what she was up to.

"Ojayjit, I don't understand why the queen is so opposed to helping Prince Mukund. He's innocent. The King of Anga wants complete control of Kshatriyapuram."

"Vedavalli, I understand your concerns. But the queen is just trying to avoid conflict with Anga. There is nothing more to it."

"Nothing more? Are you sure?"

"Yes, I am sure. The queen is doing what she thinks is best for the kingdom."

"I see," Vedavalli said. "But I still have my doubts."

"I assure you, there is nothing more to it. Trust me, Vedavalli. I have the kingdom's best interests at heart."

Vedavalli looks at him, her expression unreadable. "I hope you're right, Ojayjit. I truly hope you're right," she said.

Ojayjit nodded and then turned to leave. As he did, the light from his lamp shone into Vedavalli's eyes, and she blinked, momentarily blinded. The door closed behind him and Vedavalli was left alone in the darkness again.

CHAPTER THREE

A few days later, the annual economic development meeting with Queen Mahadevi was in progress. Vedavalli had been looking forward to this meeting for weeks, it was an opportunity for her to discuss important matters of state with the Queen and provide her with advice and counsel. On her right sat Vikramaditya, the chief advisor for education, his face a mask of concentration as he listened to the proceedings.

The Queen began the meeting, "As you know, the past few years have been difficult. Our relations with the Kingdom of Anga have had their troubles. But through it all, we have persevered. We have shown the world that the people of Malla are strong and resilient.

But we cannot rest on our laurels. We must continue to work hard to improve our economy.

Some of you may be concerned about the cost of investing in research and development. However, I believe that the long-term benefits of this investment will far outweigh the costs."

Vedavalli listened attentively as the Queen spoke, and she could see the passion and commitment in her eyes. The queen truly cared about the well-being of her kingdom and her people.

When the queen finished speaking, Vikramaditya stepped forward to present the data and statistics that supported the queen's argument. He highlighted the potential benefits of investing in research and development, and he provided concrete examples of how other kingdoms had successfully used these strategies to drive economic growth.

Vedavalli listened carefully to Vikramaditya's presentation, nodding along and adding a few suggestions of her own. The yield was improving, and more and more lands wanted black pepper and other spices.

The meeting was proceeding as planned, but while they were discussing important matters of state, Vedavalli received an urgent message from her team. They alerted her of Prince Mukund's disappearance from the infirmary. Vedavalli was shocked and confused, she didn't know what to make of this.

As she read the message further, she found out that Mukund was not alone, he had fled the palace with a girl, who was in an expensive silk saree. Vedavalli couldn't help but think that this was Ojayjit's doing.

Vedavalli waited till her agenda was discussed. She then quickly excused herself from the meeting and said to the queen and Vikramaditya, "Your Majesty, I'm sorry, but I must leave. I have received an urgent task and I must attend to it immediately."

"Of course," the queen said. "Please, take care of whatever it is that needs your attention. We can continue this discussion later."

Vedavalli nodded, and then quietly left the scene. She had to find Prince Mukund and the girl before it was too late.

CHAPTER FOUR

Avanti and Mukund were running hand in hand, trying to put as much distance between themselves and the palace as possible. They were both out of breath, but Avanti was determined to keep going. She had run away from Anga on her own for the first time, and entered Malla against her father's wishes, all for Prince Mukund.

"Mukund, you have to believe me," she said. "The Queen and her advisor, Vedavalli, are trying to kill you."

Mukund stopped running and looked at her in disbelief, "What? How do you know this?"

Avanti took a deep breath, "Ojayjit showed me. I wouldn't have believed it unless I saw it with my own eyes. He has proof, but we have to leave before sunset or else we'll be caught."

Mukund was confused, "Ojayjit? But why would he help us? I don't understand."

"He said he's been watching Vedavalli, and he knows that she's been planning to kill you ever since you arrived at the palace," Avanti replied. "He didn't want to believe it at first, but he saw the evidence with his own eyes. That's why he helped me escape with you."

Mukund was struggling to process this information. "Do you have proof? I need to see it for myself," he asked.

Mukund had heard stories about Vedavalli, known as the "The Shieldmaiden" of Malla, and he had always imagined her as a fierce and relentless leader. But after spending some time with her at the infirmary, he began to see her in a different light.

Mukund was finding it hard to reconcile his new understanding of Vedavalli as a compassionate leader, with the accusations that she was trying to kill him. He could not bring himself to believe that a person who had shown him such kindness and care would give false words or promises.

He was baffled by the accusations and thought that there must have been some mistake. He also questioned Ojayjit's true intentions and if he had other motives for helping him.

Avanti nodded, "Yes, Ojayjit gave me proof. But we have to leave now before it's too late."

Mukund hesitated for a moment, still trying to make sense of everything.

Mukund and Avanti walked throughx`x the streets of the city, their faces obscured by hoods and their clothes threadbare. They had disguised themselves as commoners in an effort to evade capture, but even still, they couldn't shake the feeling of danger that seemed to linger at their heels.

As they turned down a narrow alleyway, they caught sight of Vedavalli in the distance. She was scanning the faces of the people around her, her eyes narrowed in concentration. She was standing in the local marketplace with palace guards and the news of Prince Mukund's presence in the Malla kingdom had preceded them, as evidenced by the hushed whispers and pointed stares directed at them.

Mukund knew that she was looking for him. He couldn't risk being captured by the wrong people, but at the same time, he couldn't leave without understanding what was truly going on.

He looked at Avanti, determination in his eyes. "We'll leave, but not before I speak to Vedavalli and see the evidence for myself. I need to know the truth, no matter how difficult it may be to accept."

Avanti grabbed Mukund's arm, determined to convince him. "Ojayjit showed me the drawings with your face on them. And Vedavalli's mark," she blurted out.

"That does not mean she has orders to kill me," he told her.

"Why do you insist on her innocence?"

Mukund wanted to tell Avanti everything. About his uncle's plan to invade Kshatriyapuram, Vedavalli's insistence on a peace treaty, and his cousin's death in the conflict. But this was not the time.

"I do not trust someone who would betray their own councilwoman for the prince of a neighboring land in conflict," he said. Avanti gave in to his persistence.

As they made their way through the winding streets, they kept a watchful eye on Vedavalli's movements, always staying a few steps behind. They knew that they were getting closer to the gates, and with it, safety. But they also knew that they couldn't let their guard down. Not yet. Not until they were sure that they were out of danger.

They were just a few streets away from Vedavalli when they heard the sound of approaching soldiers. Avanti's grip on Mukund's arm tightened and she felt the tremors from the fever. He was still a sick man running for his life. They darted down another alleyway, their hearts pounding in their chests as they made a run for the palace gates.

CHAPTER FIVE

Mukund watched as a drama group approached, their costumes were bright and colorful. They were dressed as ancient gods, and he knew that this was the perfect opportunity for him and Avanti to blend in and enter the city unnoticed.

He turned to Avanti, a determined look in his eyes. "Follow my lead," he said.

Without hesitation, Mukund stepped forward and approached the group leader, who was a tall, imposing man with a booming voice. "Excuse me, sir. We are traveling performers, and we are looking for work."

The group leader looked at Mukund and Avanti. They looked tired and their clothes rumpled. "We don't need any help," he said. "We have enough performers already."

Mukund didn't give up. "Please, sir. We are very talented. We can sing, dance, and act."

"We already have a full cast."

"We would be willing to work for free" Mukund pressed.

The troupe leader paused. "Free?" he asked.

Mukund said, "Yes, sir. We're desperate to get into the capital, and we're willing to do whatever it takes."

The troupe leader stroked his beard. "Hmmm," he said. "Well, I suppose we could use some extra hands. But you'll have to prove yourselves. We're performing at the palace tonight, and you'll be on stage with us. If you can keep up, you can stay with the troupe."

Avanti quickly stepped in, "Thank you, sir! We won't let you down!"

Mukund and Avanti changed into the costumes provided by the group, Avanti's headdress for the bear was a perfect match for her saree, its dark colors and intricate patterns complementing the flowing fabric.

Soon they were marching through the streets of the capital alongside the other performers. This was a risky plan, but it was their only chance of getting inside and finding the evidence that they needed. Avanti walked beside him, her eyes scanning the crowd. She was nervous, but she trusted Mukund and knew that he had a plan.

As they approached the palace gates, Mukund's heart was in his throat. He had no idea what was waiting for them on the other side, they had to be prepared for anything.

With a deep breath, he stepped forward and entered the palace, Avanti following close behind.

The palace was abuzz with activity. Performers were milling about, setting up for the evening's show. Mukund and Avanti quickly blended in, making their way to the back of the stage. The show began, and Mukund and Avanti watched from the shadows. Mukund's eyes fell on Vedavalli as she sat under the blue silk awning, her eyes fixed on the stage as the drama unfolded.

She watched as the actors portrayed the brave acts of the Malla warriors, her mind wandering back to the past and the stories she had heard as a child.

As the performance continued, she couldn't help but notice a particular actor on stage. He was playing the role of the erstwhile king of Anga, the features very much resembling the great man everyone loved. She squinted in the dim light, trying to place him.

As the actor unleashed his sword and performed a series of acrobatic feats, Vedavalli's heart skipped a beat. She realized with a start that the actor was none other than Prince Mukund. She couldn't believe it. How had he managed to infiltrate the palace and the performance? She watched him closely, her eyes widening in surprise as he performed each daring stunt. He was unable to get up just days ago.

As he exited the scene, he saw her too, and he froze. For a moment, they just stared at each other. She waited until the crowd had dispersed, she looked over her should and realized Queen Mahadevi had recognized him too.

"Your Majesty, I believe you have recognized the performer on stage," she said in a low voice. "I suggest we handle this matter quietly, without drawing attention to ourselves."

The queen nodded, understanding the gravity of the situation. She signaled to her guards to discreetly escort Mukund to her chambers, where they could discuss the matter privately.

CHAPTER SIX

The Queen did something strange. She walked into Vedavalli's chambers, she was pacing back and forth, and her face was pale.

"Your Majesty, is there anything wrong?" Vedavalli asked.

The Queen stopped pacing and looked at Vedavalli. "I need to talk to you about Prince Mukund," she said. "I have decided to send him back."

Vedavalli was shocked. "But why?" she asked. "He is in danger in Anga Kingdom. With some reasoning, he may even side with us on the border issue. He is a reasonable man, and he knows that the border dispute is hurting both our kingdoms."

The Queen shook her head. "I know," she said. "But I cannot risk it. If we grant him asylum, it will signal a clear move against Anga. I cannot do that to my people."

Vedavalli nodded, "I understand, Your Majesty. But, if Prince Mukund is innocent, as he claims, then it means the King of Anga is planning to take over Kshatriyapuram from our control."

The queen looked at Vedavalli, her expression thoughtful. "I hear your concern, Vedavalli. But, we must also consider the safety and well-being of our kingdom. We must tread carefully and gather all the evidence before making a decision. "

"For now," the queen continued, "Let us have him as our guest. We will provide him with a safe place to stay and hear his side of the story. We will also conduct a private investigation. If he is innocent, we will help clear his name and provide him with asylum. If he is guilty, we will hand him over to the neighboring kingdom."

Vedavalli agreed, "That sounds like a fair plan, Your Majesty. I will make arrangements for Prince Mukund's stay and ensure that he is treated with the respect and hospitality befitting of a guest."

The queen nodded her approval, "Good. And Vedavalli, I trust that you will keep this matter confidential and not share it with anyone else until we have more information."

"Of course, Your Majesty," Vedavalli replied. "I will ensure that Prince Mukund's presence in the palace remains a secret until we have all the facts."

It was a quiet night at the palace, and most of the residents were asleep. But in the guest room where Prince Mukund was staying, he felt the silence deafening. His beloved Avanti was asleep in a guest room in the women's quarters. It was the middle of the night when the attack came. The sound of shattering pottery echoed through the halls as an intruder broke the window and entered his room.

Mukund was caught off guard, but he quickly sprang into action.

"Who are you?" he shouted. "What do you want?" he asked the one whose hood had partially fallen revealing his eyes.

He grabbed a nearby candlestick and swung it at the intruder, striking them on the head. The intruder stumbled, but quickly regained their footing and tried to search the room.

Soon more entered and were trying to keep Mukund down while searching for something. Mukund's stitches tore open and blood oozed. They were interrupted by the sound of guards running down the hallway. They quickly fled, leaving Mukund lying on the floor, unconscious and bleeding.

When Mukund woke up, he was lying on the floor, still bleeding. The men were gone, and the room was a mess. There were broken pots and furniture scattered everywhere.

Mukund tried to get up, but he was too weak. He crawled to the door and tried to open it, but it was locked. He pounded on the door and shouted for help, but no one came. Overwhelmed by blood loss, he grew dizzy and collapsed, the blood seeping under the door.

A few minutes later, a guard who was patrolling the hallway noticed the blood outside Mukund's room and knocked on the door. When there was no answer, he broke open the door and saw Mukund lying on the floor, bleeding profusely. The guard rushed into the room, shouting to the nearby guards to help carry Mukund to the infirmary.

Upon hearing the news, Vedavalli arrived at the scene. The door to the room was ajar, and Vedavalli could see that the window had been broken. "Is he conscious?", she asked the chief guard standing next to her. He shook his head and looked down. She wasted no time in running to the infirmary.

She knelt beside him, her eyes scanning his injuries, taking in the cuts and bruises that covered his body. A mix of emotions swirled within her, and she murmured under her breath, "I only wanted to scare you," regret seeping into her voice. She glanced around, ensuring no one overheard her vulnerable confession.

Things had gone out of control. Her setup had been perfect, including the plan to make him go against the King. She had intended to inflict fear, not irreparable harm.

CHAPTER SEVEN

Avanti sat on the floor, tears streaming down her face as she received the news of Prince Mukund's passing. She couldn't believe that he was gone, and she was unable to accept the sense of loss and grief. She sobbed as she thought about all the things she would never get to say to Mukund.

"My fault," she said. "I allowed him to come back here, to the place that wants to kill him."

"I should have refused to accept the hospitality, taken him far away into the forests."

She pounded her fists on the ground in anger and frustration. "Avanti," Vedavalli said, kneeling down next to her. "I'm so sorry."

Avanti looked up at her, her eyes red and swollen. "He's gone," she said. "He's really gone."

Vedavalli put her arms around Avanti and hugged her tightly. "I know," she said. "I'm so sorry." Vedavalli did not know what to say to the grieving. Having lost her mother so young, she was uncomfortable around death. She felt like she didn't have the right words to comfort Avanti.

Avanti requested Queen Mahadevi to arrange for her journey back to Anga kingdom, as she didn't want to stay in Malla kingdom any longer. She couldn't bear to be in a place where Mukund was no longer alive.

The Queen granted her request and arranged for her safe passage back to Anga. Vedavalli watched Avanti go, and she felt a wave of guilt wash over her. She was conflicted about her actions, but she had done it for Avanti's own good. Avanti was escorted by a team of guards, who were under the orders of Vedavalli, to make sure Avanti would be safe on her journey.

The capital was still abuzz with the news of Prince Mukund's passing, but unknown to most, he was alive and recovering in a secret room below Vedavalli's chambers. With his face bandaged and body covered in blankets, he appeared to be in pain and his breathing was labored.

Prince Mukund confided in Vedavalli about his concerns for Avanti's safety. "I am worried she will hurt herself," he told her.

Vedavalli understood his concerns but to uncover the truth about Prince Rajesh's death they had to make it look like Prince Mukund was no longer a threat.

The only attacker they managed to capture was being interrogated without the council's approval. Vedavalli watched as he strained against the chains, his muscles burning with effort, sweat pouring down his face.

"How did you get into the fort?" she asked.

The attacker hesitated, the chains tightened around him. He slowly reached out to his inner pocket and then held out a ring.

Vedavalli's pretended to be surprised as she saw Queen Mahadevi's signet ring. "How did you get that?" she asked.

The attacker didn't answer. He just stared at the ring in his hand. If the attacker had the queen's ring, then it meant that someone within the palace was involved in the attack.

Vedavalli guessed others must have escaped from the fort through the secret passage that leads out from the royal bath of the palace.

How did they have knowledge of the secret passages?

A week later, Mukund was dressed in plain clothes, his face still bandaged from his injuries. Despite his appearance, his eyes held a determination that Vedavalli recognized all too well.

"Welcome to the team, Officer Prithviraj," she said, inclining her head in greeting. A small smile played on her lips.

Mukund bowed his head in return. "Thank you, Vedavalli. I won't let you down."

Vedavalli nodded a small smile on her face. As Officer Prithviraj, he can access places and approach people that would have been off-limits to him as the Prince of Anga. Who killed Prince Rajesh and framed Mukund? What has it got to do with the border issue? So many questions and no answers.

Mukund's thoughts were interrupted by Vedavalli. "We need to get started," she said. "There's a lot of work to do."

CHAPTER EIGHT

Vedavalli and Prince Mukund arrived at the border of Kshatriyapuram. Vedavalli got down from her caravan, she stared at the setting sun. They were on time, but she couldn't shake off the feeling of unease as they approached the village. She had rejected the idea of riding horseback from the palace to Kshatriyapuram, as she knew that it would only add to the already tense atmosphere. She even switched her official clothing to make the villagers feel friendly.

As they made their way through the village, they were greeted by curious and wary glances from the villagers. Kshatriyapuram was a tight-knit community of farmers, artisans, and merchants. Vedavalli knew that her father's influence was strong in the village, as he was the head of the council of elders, deeply respected by the villagers. The village was also known for its skilled archers and warriors, who were trained from a young age to defend the village from any external threats.

They made their way to the village council's meeting hall, where the meeting with the village leaders was to take place. Vedavalli's father was already seated at the head of the table. He acknowledged Vedavalli with a nod, but his expression was cold and distant.

Vedavalli sat in the council meeting hall, her gaze fixed on the door as she waited for the elders to arrive. She fidgeted with her hands, her thoughts preoccupied with her conversation with the Queen. A worried look was etched on her face, her mind clearly troubled as she remembered the Queen's warning.

"Are you sure you're ready for this? Your father is a difficult man, and he doesn't always see eye to eye with our kingdom's policies."

"I understand, Your Majesty. But it is my duty to ensure the safety and well-being of all the people in our kingdom, including those in Kshatriyapuram. I will do whatever it takes to resolve this border dispute, even if it means facing my own personal demons."

Vedavalli's thoughts turned to her personal demons. She knew that she had to face them if she was to succeed in her mission. Even if it meant revisiting her father's disapproval, her own doubts, and the tragedy that had broken her family.

"I have faith in you, Vedavalli. You are a strong and capable leader. Now, you have Officer Prithviraj with you, and he is a skilled warrior and a valuable asset to your team. Remember, we are still not sure who is behind the false accusations against him and we cannot take any chances. Keep him close and trust only those who you know you can trust."

As the council meeting began, Vedavalli took her seat next to the head of the table. The elders of Kshatriyapuram had arranged a lengthy table adorned with numerous food platters and water jugs for the Anga people, then settled themselves at the adjacent, shorter table. Despite the hospitality, the atmosphere in the room was tense, as both sides were determined to make their case heard.

The leader of the Kshatriyapuram council, Vedavalli's father, was the first to speak. "This land has been in our possession for generations. It is crucial to our farming operations and the livelihoods of our villagers. We cannot allow the neighboring kingdom of Anga to take it from us."

The representative from Anga, a tall man with a stern expression, stood up to respond. "We understand the importance of the land to your village, but it is also important to our kingdom's expansion and development. We have been negotiating in good faith, but it seems that Kshatriyapuram is unwilling to come to a compromise."

The argument continued back and forth, with both sides presenting evidence and making their case. Vedavalli listened carefully, taking note of the key points and concerns raised by both sides.

Meanwhile, Mukund had blended in with the common folk and was keeping a low profile, but she knew that he was keenly observing the proceedings. She also noticed that he had spotted the Anga flag and was on high alert. His regal bearing was betrayed only by the hint of nervousness in the way he held himself. No one seemed to identify him.

Vedavalli realized that this would work in their favor as they could move around the village with more freedom and gather information without drawing attention to themselves.

As the meeting came to a close, Vedavalli turned to Prithviraj and whispered, "You did well, officer. Keep up the good work." He nodded in response, his eyes scanning the room as they made their way out of the council hall. She knew that he would be vigilant and would not let his guard down, knowing that the safety of himself and the village is at stake.

As night fell on Kshatriyapuram, Prince Mukund stood outside Vedavalli's living quarters, lost in thought. He had been away from his kingdom for twenty nights, and he was beginning to miss it. He was patient and observant, carefully studied his environment, and adjusted his behavior accordingly. Kshatriyapuram in many ways reminded him of Suvarna, the capital of Anga.

When he saw the ambassadors of Anga arrive at the council to discuss the land dispute, he was taken aback. He accidentally came close to a group of soldiers protecting the ambassadors. One of them looked at him suspiciously. Mukund felt his heart skip a beat, and he quickened his pace, hoping to lose himself in the throngs of people.

"Come in", a female voice brought him back to the present. He made his way to the veranda where they could speak in public without causing whispers.

Vedavalli was accustomed to emergencies occurring during the night. Although it wasn't unusual for officers or messengers to visit her, this was the first time Mukund had come to see her privately. She couldn't shake the feeling that they were being observed.

"Is everything alright, Officer Prithviraj?" she asked, trying to keep her tone formal.

Mukund hesitated for a moment, Vedavalli took the initiative and addressed the elephant in the room.

"As a servant of Anga, Prince Mukund, what do you think?" Vedavalli said in a hushed tone, as she knew they might be overheard. She wanted his insight on the matter as a prince and someone who understands the politics of both kingdoms.

Mukund thought for a moment before responding. "I think that both kingdoms should come to a compromise that benefits both parties. The land is crucial for the livelihood of the villagers here, but it also holds strategic importance for Anga's expansion. Perhaps a joint venture or shared use of the land could be negotiated."

Vedavalli was intrigued by Mukund's suggestion, but she needed more details. "How would that work, Mukund? Who would own the land? Malla or Anga?"

Mukund leaned forward as he spoke. "It could be owned jointly by both kingdoms, with a council of representatives from both sides to manage it. The land could be used for farming by the villagers here, but also for expansion and development by Anga. The council would ensure that the land is used sustainably and that the rights of both parties are respected."

Vedavalli listened intently, " I had something similar in mind. Having both kingdoms fight over this land is not useful. I will propose this in the council meeting tomorrow and see if it can be negotiated with the elders. "

She realized she was sitting too close to him and they had not broken eye contact. She felt her cheeks flush as she stepped back and turned away, trying to compose herself. Vedavalli was surprised by Mukund's concern for the people, as he was a prince from a neighboring kingdom, and his loyalty was to Anga, not Malla.

She walked Mukund to the door, and they said their goodbyes. As she watched him go, she couldn't help but smile. She had a feeling that this was just the beginning of a long and fruitful partnership.

As Mukund returned to his room, he couldn't stop thinking about his conversation with Vedavalli. He was impressed by her intelligence and her willingness to listen to his ideas.

The accounts he had heard of her in Anga's courtroom were otherwise. They painted her as a cold, ruthless, and calculating advisor who would do whatever it takes to get what she wants. But now, as he spent more time with her, he saw a different side of her. He saw a woman who was compassionate and made sure everyone makes the best of an opportunity.

CHAPTER NINE

The next day, Vedavalli and Mukund set out to explore the village of Kshatriyapuram. They walked through the streets, talking to the villagers and getting a better understanding of their concerns and needs.

They also took the opportunity to observe the village's archery training. Vedavalli was impressed by the skill and discipline of the trainees, and she could see that the village had a strong tradition of defending itself. Mukund, who was a skilled archer himself, joined in on the training and impressed the villagers with his own abilities.

As they spent more time together, Vedavalli began to notice a subtle shift in the way Mukund interacted with the villagers. He seemed genuinely interested in their well-being, and was not afraid to speak his mind, even when it went against her own opinions.

It dawned on her that despite their different backgrounds, they shared a common goal: to serve and protect the people of their kingdom.

The sun was setting and the sky was painted in warm hues of orange and pink. Prince Mukund was standing by the lake, the water rippling with the wind. He was young and handsome and very much the way Vedavalli had imagined him to be when she first heard of him. Vedavalli and Mukund stood side by side, watching the sunset, lost in their own thoughts.

"Did the elders agree to another meeting?"

"Yes, they did. It was not easy, but I had to promise that the village's interests will be protected." Vedavalli replied, her tone guarded.

Mukund nodded understandingly, "I know it can be difficult when family is involved in matters of state. But you have to put the needs of your kingdom first."

Vedavalli looks at him, surprised, "How did you know?"

"You mentioned having to face one person in particular. Also, I could tell from the way you interacted with him yesterday. You looked down the whole time, your shoulders slumped and you never made eye contact" Mukund replied with a small smile. "He reminds me of my own father. The way he looks at you, the way he speaks to you. It's clear that there's a history there."

Vedavalli felt a pang of sadness, but she nodded in understanding. "Yes, we have our differences. But I love him, and I know he loves me too. It's just hard for him to accept that I have chosen a different path."

"I understand," Mukund said, reaching out to give her hand a reassuring squeeze. "But I have faith that you will find a way to reconcile with him. You're a strong and capable woman, Vedavalli. You can do anything."

Her heart fluttered at the genuine warmth in his eyes. She had to remind herself that he was still a prince, and she was still an advisor.

As they stood together watching the sunset, Mukund suddenly spoke;

"You know, Vedavalli," he said, his voice tinged with wistfulness, "Avanti and I have been through so much together. When we first met, I was so nervous that I hid the fact that I was a prince."

Vedavalli felt a deep ravine open up between them. She listened intently, her heart heavy as she realized that she may have been the only one feeling a connection between them.

Mukund was still thinking about Avanti and the love he had for her. As he spoke of Avanti, Vedavalli felt the weight of disappointment settle in her chest like a heavy stone, threatening to upset her careful balance. Vedavalli tried to push down the feeling of disappointment and instead focused on being a good listener and support for Mukund.

CHAPTER TEN

Vedavalli gently rapped her knuckles against the door, but no one answered. She tried again, but still, there was no response. Her gaze surveyed the intricate wood carvings on the door, which had withstood the passage of time.

Just as she was about to knock for the third time, the door slowly creaked open. Her father stood in front of her, his expression just as inscrutable as it was when she had left to work at the palace nine years ago. He gave a small nod and stepped aside, allowing her to enter. Nothing had changed. Despite every effort, nothing had changed!

Taking in her surroundings, Vedavalli felt as though she were a stranger in someone else's home. The interior had undergone a series of changes since she had last been there. Her childhood bedroom, once filled with toys, was now pristine, with everything packed away in a trunk.

Feeling lost, Vedavalli made her way over to the swing and sat down, unsure of what to say or ask. It was only after a long moment of silence that she finally managed to speak.

"How are you, Appa?" she asked, her gaze focused on the small plant in the corner of the room.

Her father's response was delayed, and when he did finally speak, his voice was flat and devoid of emotion. "I'm fine, thank you," he said. "And how are you, Vedavalli?"

"I'm well, thank you," she replied.

For a while, they sat in silence, Vedavalli unsure of what to say or do. Her father didn't offer any conversation, and Vedavalli was hesitant to pry. It was only when she spotted a picture of her mother on the wall that she felt compelled to speak.

"I miss Amma," she said softly, her voice cracking with emotion.

Her father's expression softened slightly, and he nodded in agreement. "Yes," he said. "I miss her very much too."

There was something they needed to talk about, some unresolved tension that hung between them like a heavy fog. When she couldn't take it anymore, "I have the treaty ready. We can discuss it tomorrow at the council."

He nodded once. She stood up to leave.

A single tear rolled down her cheek. Even after all these years and all the things he had done, she realized she still loved her father. As soon as she stepped outside, she was caught off guard by the sight of Mukund's face.

"Vedavalli, you need to come," he said, his voice urgent.

Mukund's tone was unusual, and she wondered what could be so important.

"What's wrong?" she asked.

"It's the market," Mukund said, his eyes troubled. "Something's happening"

Shouts and screams filled the air, and the sounds of clashing weapons echoed through the streets. The prince and the advisor rushed outside to see what was happening, and they were met with a chaotic scene.

A group of villagers had gathered in the center of the village, wielding sticks and pitchforks, and were facing off against a squad of soldiers from the neighboring kingdom.

The soldiers were trying to collect taxes from the villagers, but the villagers were refusing to pay, insisting that they were being unfairly burdened.

As they watched, a young girl ran out of one of the nearby houses, screaming at the top of her lungs. One of the soldiers reached out to grab her, but she slipped away and ran to the crowds.

That was the moment when the situation exploded. One of the villagers raised his pitchfork and charged toward the soldiers, and the others quickly followed suit. The air was filled with the sound of clanging metal, shouting, and the screams of the wounded.

Vedavalli and Mukund exchanged a glance. "We need to find a way to separate them," Vedavalli said, her voice filled with determination.

Mukund nodded in agreement. "I'll distract the soldiers. You get the villagers to safety."

Vedavalli didn't hesitate. She quickly made her way toward the villagers, who were locked in combat with the soldiers. She shouted at them, urging them to stop fighting and move to safety.

"Come with me!" she yelled. "We need to get out of here!"

Some of the villagers hesitated, still caught up in the heat of battle, but Vedavalli kept at it. She grabbed one of the women by the arm and pulled her toward the safety of a nearby building.

Meanwhile, Mukund managed to get the attention of the soldiers. He ran towards them, waving his arms and shouting. The soldiers turned towards him, their weapons raised.

But Mukund wasn't intimidated. He kept running towards them, dodging their attacks and shouting insults. The soldiers were so focused on him that they didn't even notice when the villagers slipped away.

Finally, Vedavalli and Mukund managed to get everyone to safety. They took the villagers to a nearby temple, where they could rest and recover from their injuries.

As they tended to the wounded and helped the villagers calm down, Vedavalli and Mukund couldn't help but discuss what they had just witnessed.

"I can't believe both kingdoms are engaging in tax collection," Vedavalli said, shaking her head in disbelief. "The villagers were right to resist."

Mukund nodded in agreement. "It's a shame that the common people have to bear the brunt of the greed. We need to do something about it."

Vedavalli looked at Mukund. "You're right. We can't let this go on any longer. We need to bring this to the attention of the Queen."

Mukund nodded. "I'll prepare a report detailing what we saw today. We can present it to the Queen and urge her to take action against those responsible for this illegal tax collection."

As a sense of purpose washed over her, she forgot all about the sad memories from her childhood.

CHAPTER ELEVEN

The first light of dawn illuminated the grand palace gates as Vedavalli and Mukund approached, their horses' hooves stirring up dust and dirt from the ground.

News had reached the Queen of Malla about Anga's construction of a memorial for Mukund's cousin in the capital Survarna. However, she was not invited to the ceremony, as Anga had taken offense to her providing shelter to Mukund "when he was alive." It appeared that Anga had forgotten about their prince, but have they really forgiven him? Not quite.

When Vedavalli and Mukund both returned back to the palace of Malla, some of the soldiers were eyeing Mukund suspiciously as if they recognized the officer in Vedavalli's team. Even without the jewelry and colorful upper drapes, Mukund stood out in his simple cotton attire.

"I have news," Ojayjit said hesitantly, motioning for Vedavalli to follow him.

Vedavalli gestured for Mukund to wait outside. A cool breeze swept through the hall, carrying with it the scent of blooming flowers from the nearby gardens.

Once inside, Ojayjit spoke, "King Rajiv of Anga has welcomed his heir. It might not be long before he proposes a marriage between his heir and our Queen's youngest when they're of age."

A lump formed in Vedavalli's throat. There were countless ways that things could go wrong if Mukund's survival was discovered. Later that evening, she requested a walk with Mukund. The leaves on the trees rustled gently in the evening breeze, creating a soothing, rhythmic sound.

Vedavalli's demeanor grew increasingly serious. Finally, as they turned a corner and entered a small antechamber, she stopped and turned to Mukund, her expression grave.

"Prithviraj, I have news," she said, her voice low and urgent.

"What is it?" he asked, bracing himself for the worst.

"He has a son. The King of Anga. A healthy, male heir," Vedavalli said, his eyes fixed on Mukund's face.

"I see," Mukund said, his voice tinged with sadness. "Another son for my uncle. He must be overjoyed."

Vedavalli nodded sympathetically. "I'm sorry, Prithviraj. I know this must be hard for you. But we cannot lose hope. We will find a way to clear your name and restore your rightful place on the throne."

"Yes we will" he murmured quietly.

"Ahem.." they heard someone clear their throat nearby and noticed Ojayjit walking towards them. Immediately they both moved away from each other. Putting distance to that proximity they didn't know had inhabited them.

"I will speak to you later" she spoke loudly, Mukund bowed before leaving her alone.

"You have become friendly with strangers, in all my years here I've never seen you allow any official near you."

Vedavalli's eyes flared in anger.

"What are you accusing me of?" she demanded.

"Nothing, dear Vedavalli. Just conveying what I observed. Friendly relations with comrades in arms are a positive trait."

Ojayjit was smiling, but it was not a friendly one. His words never meant what he thought or felt.

Mukund didn't move from his place as he saw Vedavalli and Ojayjit walk away. He found himself a bench to sit on.

"Prithviraj," her voice reverberated in his mind, a gentle melody that brought forth a flood of memories. The way she enunciated his formal name, now that they were amidst people who recognized him as Mukund, stirred a kaleidoscope of emotions within him. It seemed like she had grown distant as if something bothered her and as if they had not become comrades during their time together in the village.

Mukund's mind flashed back to memories of his cousin Rajesh, the one he was accused of killing. He remembered how they used to play together as children, how they would run through the fields and swim in the river. Rajesh had been like a brother to him, and now he was gone. All the deaths he had seen made him a little more cynical every day.

A trait he shared with Vedavalli. Earlier when they spoke, Vedavalli's eyes were empty, unlike her words, as if something had broken her inside.

CHAPTER TWELVE

Meanwhile, in Anga, celebrations were in full swing. The newborn had brought in new hope for their kingdom. Now the need to find and kill Mukund had been muted by joy; the farmers celebrated the season as if it was a bountiful harvest.

Avanti was still grieving her lover, feeling as though a part of her had been torn away and lost forever, like a bird with a broken wing unable to soar. Her father kept banging on her door; a drumbeat, relentless and unyielding. When she opened it hesitatingly, he barged into her room, a fierce wind, disturbing the stillness.

"There is a boy from the east, he has agreed to marry you," he announced.

"Appa, you do not understand. He was innocent."

"Quiet child. If anyone finds out you knew Prince Mukund, you will be hurled with stones and sticks every time you leave the house. That murderer has no place here," her father warned.

"You met him! You fed him! You still think he murdered his own family?" she yelled through the tears, like a thunderstorm lashing out at the earth.

Her father hesitated a moment but continued.

"It does not matter what I think. The crown believes it, and we are a part of it," he concluded.

Avanti lay in her defeated position weeping, dressed in her finest silk saree, waiting for the prospective groom to arrive.

The sound of footsteps alerted her to the arrival of a young man dressed in a simple white kurta and dhoti.

"I am Keshav," he said, bringing his palms together and bowing to greet.

Avanti nodded but didn't smile. She had no intention of pretending to be interested in this meeting.

They sat across from each other at a wooden table, decorated with plates of sweets and fruit. Avanti picked at the food, barely tasting it.

"So, Avanti, your father tells me you are a skilled musician," Keshav said, attempting to make conversation. Those words took her to a time when music had brought her joy instead of pain. She remembered playing the veena for Prince Mukund, the way he had leaned in close to listen, the way his eyes had glinted with appreciation.

Avanti shrugged. "It's a hobby."

"I enjoy music. Perhaps you could play something for me later?"

Avanti shook her head. "I don't think so."

The conversation stalled, and Avanti felt like she was suffocating. She glanced up at Keshav, and something about his expression caught her attention. His eyes seemed to be searching hers, looking for something.

"Why are you here?" she blurted out, unable to contain her suspicion any longer.

Keshav hesitated for a moment, then leaned forward. "I'm sorry, Avanti. I didn't want to deceive you, but I had no choice. I was sent here by the king's advisor to gather information about your family's involvement with Prince Mukund's case."

"What will you do with the information?" she asked, her voice barely above a whisper.

"I don't know yet. But I promise you, Avanti, I won't hurt you or your family. I only took this job because I needed the money."

"I won't tell you anything," she said firmly.

"But sometimes the truth has a way of revealing itself", Keshav was warning her that the truth would eventually emerge, no matter how hard she tried to bury it.

"I don't know what you're talking about," she said, trying to sound convincing.

Keshav's expression softened. "I'm not trying to threaten you, Avanti. I just want to help. If there's anything you need, anything at all, you can come to me."

And with that, he stood up, his broad frame casting a shadow over Avanti.

"I should be going," Keshav said, his voice tinged with regret.

"Remember, your secret is safe with me", and the door closed behind him.

Keshav walked up to the end of the street before turning into an alley.

"What did she say?" asked a voice urgently.

"She is afraid. I will make her give up the truth," he told the veiled woman standing opposite him.

"And bury this." she lowered her voice abruptly handing over a small package wrapped in silk.

Keshav turned to both sides looking for any eavesdroppers before taking it from her hand.

"No one should know what happened to Prince Rajesh."

Keshav nodded gravely, tucking the package inside his coat. He had been tasked with finding out the truth about Prince Mukund's disappearance and sudden death, and it seemed like he was getting closer to the answers he sought.

The veiled woman quickly disappeared into the shadows. Keshav watched her go before turning back towards the street. He couldn't afford to be seen with her. Secrecy was important to his work as a private investigator, and his job was to find out the truth, no matter how ugly it might be.

Once he reached his office, Keshav closed the door behind him and took out the package. It was small and light, but he could feel something solid inside. He carefully unwrapped the silk and gasped when he saw what was inside.

When the mysterious woman first approached him with a huge sum for any news on Avanti, he decided to start by looking into Prince Mukund, the man who had been blamed for Prince Rajesh's death.

Keshav spent the next few days gathering information about Prince Mukund. He learned that the prince had indeed been on the run, trying to clear his name. But unfortunately, he had been killed in a supposed encounter with some soldiers-for-hire. Keshav suspected foul play, and he was determined to find out who was behind it.

CHAPTER THIRTEEN

Keshav continued maintaining his distance from Avanti in the hopes of getting her to reveal what she knows about the happenings in Malla. But she didn't.

Frustrated and out of ideas, Keshav decided to take a break from his investigation and clear his mind. And that's when it happened, as he took his usual walk to the park, an alley begged his attention and there lay the corpse, the veiled woman, his client, dead in bright sunlight.

His heart pounded, he was drowning in a sea of uncertainty, and if he called the royal police, they would detect their connection.,

Just then he noticed a small package she was clenching in her hands, like a key to the mystery. It could be something that caused her death. He quietly wrapped his fingers around the clothing in his dhoti and picked up the package.

You are not a thief, you are solving a murder, helping a person he reassured himself.

He then walked hurriedly to the royal men in uniform at the park end and informed them of the corpse.

The next few days were a blur for Keshav. He couldn't stop thinking about the veiled woman's death and what it meant for his investigation. Whoever had employed her was now high on his list of suspects. The fact that they had silenced her only reinforced his belief that they were covering their tracks.

Keshav spent hours poring over the information he had gathered, trying to find any leads that could help him identify the person behind the veiled woman's death. But the more he dug, the more he felt like he was hitting a dead end. It was as if someone had gone to great lengths to ensure that there was no trace left behind.

As he looked at the small package he had stolen from the veiled woman's hands. He knew that it could hold the key to unraveling the mystery surrounding Prince Mukund's death, but he was hesitant to open it.

It was like standing at the edge of a cliff, looking down at the unknown depths below. He didn't know what he would find inside the package, and that made him nervous. But he also knew that he couldn't afford to let his fears hold him back, it was a risk he had to take. He needed to know what was inside.

Keshav's hands were steady as he wrapped a piece of his worn-out dhoti around his fingers like a guard, making sure not to damage the package. He began to carefully unknot the pouch, unraveling the silk with great care.

As he peeled away the layers of silk, he could almost taste the adrenaline pumping through his veins. He knew that he was close to uncovering the truth about Prince Mukund's death.

Finally, he reached the final layer of silk, and as he pulled it away, he gasped in disbelief at what he saw. Inside the pouch was a small, intricately designed piece of paper. On it, in elegant handwriting, was a single word: "Avanti."

The veiled woman knew she was going to be killed, so the paper was indeed for him, she was coming to see Keshav and it was a clue she left for him.

CHAPTER FOURTEEN

Avanti knew she was being watched, she gripped the basket of vegetables tightly. It was supposed to be a joyful day, the air was filled with the smell of ghee from the sweet stalls, but Avanti felt restless.

She knew that her paranoia was a result of the recent events that had unfolded in her life, but she couldn't help feeling like she was being followed. She noticed a man with a golden armband and silky waistband standing at the end of the alleyway, his eyes fixed on her. She sped up, dodged people carrying baskets on their heads, and turned in directions to confuse the man who was following her—all at once.

As she darted through the twisting streets and alleys, she could hear the sounds of the men in pursuit, their footsteps pounding on the cobblestones. But she pushed herself harder, running faster than she ever had before, driven by fear and desperation.

Finally, after what felt like an eternity, she stumbled into a narrow alleyway, her breath coming in ragged gasps. She leaned against the wall, her heart pounding in her chest, and tried to catch her breath.

She felt a hand grab her shoulder. She spun around, her heart racing, to find Keshav standing there, concern etched on his face. "Avanti, are you okay?" Keshav asked, his voice low and urgent. "You need to come with me, it's not safe here."

As they moved through the alley, Avanti could feel the weight of Keshav's gaze on her, and she knew that he was searching for something in her eyes. She could tell that he was suspicious and was trying to get her to reveal what she knew.

But Avanti was determined not to give in. She had her own secrets, her own reasons for staying silent, and she wasn't about to let Keshav or anyone else get in the way of her plans.

Suddenly, a loud commotion broke out behind them, and Avanti turned to see a group of men in dark robes charging at them. Keshav grabbed her hand and pulled her toward the end of the alley, but the men were gaining on them fast.

Keshav pulled out a small knife from his dhoti and held it out in front of him, ready to defend them both as they ran.

Finally, Keshav forced open a small rusted door, allowing them to enter a dark room riddled with cobwebs.

Keshav and Avanti cautiously stepped into the dark room covered in cobwebs, their eyes struggling to adjust to the dimness. They could hear the sound of their own breathing and the rustling of the cobwebs as they brushed past them.

The air was thick with the musty smell of age, reminding her of old furniture, broken pottery, and dusty books.

Avanti couldn't help but shudder as she looked around the room. She had never been in a place like this before, and it made her feel uneasy.

Keshav put his finger over his lips, signaling her not to make any noise until they know they were not pursued.

Avanti nodded slightly, it was difficult to make out her expression in the dark. They waited there, crouching, listening to the sound of their pursuers' footsteps getting closer and closer. The men were getting louder, their voices echoing through the narrow alleyway.

Keshav gestured for Avanti to move back further into the room, and they crept silently along the wall until they were hidden in the shadows. They could see the silhouettes of the men as they approached the door, their voices growing louder.

Suddenly, one of the men stopped. Keshav held his breath, hoping that they wouldn't be discovered. The man paused for a moment, then shook his head and continued on, his companions following close behind.

Keshav and Avanti waited until they could no longer hear the sound of the men's footsteps echoing through the alleyway. Only then did Keshav let out a sigh of relief, signaling to Avanti that it was safe to move.

They carefully made their way back to the door and peered outside, scanning the area for any sign of their pursuers. When they were certain that the coast was clear, they stepped out into the alleyway and began to make their way back to Keshav's office.

Upon entering his office, Keshav did a thorough search to ensure no one was waiting to attack him. He moved cautiously around the room, scanning every corner with his sharp eyes. The silence in the room was deafening, but Keshav's instincts were on high alert. He knew that danger could lurk in even the most unexpected places.

Finally, after satisfying himself that the room was secure, Keshav turned to face Avanti. She looked frail and scared, her eyes wide with fear. Keshav could see the tension in her muscles as if she was ready to bolt at any moment.

He handed her a small pot, his expression sympathetic. "Drink this," he said softly. "You need to calm down."

Avanti took a few deep breaths and drank the water. She then looked up at Keshav, her eyes pleading for answers.

"How did you know I was there?" she asked, her voice barely above a whisper.

Keshav sighed. "I was following you, and for that, I am sorry. It was clear from our first meeting that you were hiding something. And... the person who employed me to find you was killed this morning."

Avanti's eyes widened in shock, and she gasped softly. Her hands began to tremble, and she clutched at her chest as if trying to hold herself together.

"Killed?" she whispered. "Who would do such a thing?"

"That's what I am trying to find out," Keshav replied, pulling out the small piece of paper. "But before she died, the veiled woman gave me a package with your name on it."

Avanti's hand shook as she took the paper from Keshav's hand. She stared at the single word written on it, her expression unreadable.

"You know this woman?" Keshav asked gently.

Avanti shook her head slightly as if to say no, but Keshav could see the fear in her eyes. He knew that she was hiding something, something important.

"Avanti," Keshav said, his voice firm. "You need to trust me. Tell me everything you know. I will protect you, I promise."

Avanti's eyes filled with tears, and she looked up at Keshav, her expression vulnerable. "Promise on your life, the ones you love, that you will help me," she said.

Keshav nodded solemnly. "I promise," he said, his eyes meeting hers. "I will do everything in my power to keep you safe."

Without protection, she knew she would also die.

50

CHAPTER FIFTEEN

Vedavalli arrived at the border of Anga waiting for the troops to let her in. The baskets covered in silk were an indication that she had arrived for the naming ceremony of the heir. They contained gifts for the newborn prince, as well as offerings for the royal family, beautifully decorated with flowers and ribbons.

Kingdoms flaunted their wealth and prosperity through gifts. Queen Mahadevi had insisted the jewelers make heavy lockets encrusted with stones like ruby and emerald for the child.

As she waited, Vedavalli looked around her, taking in the sights and sounds of the border town much similar to Kshatriyapuram bustling with activity. But Kshatriyapuram had a different story to tell, unlike this one where Anga held complete control.

Her thoughts turned back to the present when the carriage finally reached the palace gates. She was excited to be in Anga, and she was grateful for the opportunity to witness the naming ceremony of the heir. When Malla held a naming ceremony for their princess a few weeks back she had been in Kshatriyapuram unearthing corruption. She wondered how many towns and villages across the kingdom were suffering from similar injustices, and how many people were struggling to make ends meet.

Today, she had a purpose, a reason to keep the attention on her. The Queen of Malla had reluctantly approved Vedavalli's plan to sneak into his erstwhile chambers Mukund during the ceremony.

"Too many risks."

"I don't know how long it will take for me to get you out if they held you captive for letting in a traitor." she shook her head and threw her hands as if thinking of the effort troubled her.

To find any clues, Mukund must be inside the royal quarters.

Despite the high stakes and a short window of opportunity, Vedavalli and Mukund meticulously planned the operation. Vedavalli would distract the guards and courtiers by presenting gifts and offerings to the royal family while Mukund sneaked into his erstwhile chambers — a delicate dance.

As it began, Vedavalli made her way to the dais where the royal family sat. She bowed before Queen Meenakshi and presented the gifts, and then made her way to the cradle where the newborn prince lay. She whispered a silent prayer for the safety and prosperity of the young prince . As she walked, her anklets clinked softly against the granite steps.

She began to recite a poem she had written, drawing the attention of the guests towards her. Reciting, she moved towards the prince's chambers like a choreographed play, forcing the guards to focus on her.

Before she could blink, the poem ended, and she had no idea if he had made out safely. Prior to returning to her seat, she paused, waiting for the King and Queen of Anga to react, and breathed out only when she heard clapping.

As the naming ceremony of the prince in Anga came to an end, Vedavalli felt a sense of relief wash over her. She had managed to distract the guards and courtiers long enough for Mukund to sneak in unnoticed. She prayed he would find the exit passage as planned.

But as she made her way towards the exit, she was suddenly surrounded by guards.

"We need to check your belongings, shieldmaiden"

"On what grounds sir?"

"There is a necklace missing from the display this morning, and all guests are being checked as a precaution."

Vedavalli had to allow them. They looked through her belongings, including her clothes, her jewelry, and her books.

After a few minutes, the guards found the jewel. It was a beautiful piece of jewelry, encrusted with diamonds and rubies.

"This is it!" one of the guards said triumphantly. "This is the jewel that was stolen from the treasury."

Vedavalli gasped. "That's not mine!" she said. "I've never seen that jewel before in my life."

The guards didn't believe her. "We found it in your belongings," one of them said. "That's proof that you stole it."

"I'm telling you, I didn't steal it!" Vedavalli said. "Someone must have planted it in my belongings.

Through anger and frustration she refused to back down, her voice firm as she defended herself. "No, I am the advisor to the Queen of Malla," she said, her words echoing off the cold, stone walls. "I care more than anyone about diplomatic relations between our kingdoms."

But it was no use. The guards were not interested in her words, only in following orders. The chief barked out a command, his voice sharp and cutting like the crack of a whip.

"Take her away," he ordered, and one of the lady guards seized Vedavalli roughly.

She couldn't help but feel like a fish caught in a net, struggling to break free but unable to escape the inevitable fate.

The sound of her footsteps echoed through the corridors of the palace, the tolling of a funeral bell, announcing the end of her freedom.

She could smell the musty odor of the prison cells, a damp and suffocating smell that seemed to permeate her clothes and hair as if it was trying to remind her of her confinement.

As she sat in her cell, waiting for what felt like an eternity, Vedavalli couldn't help but wonder if this was the end of her journey, or if there was still a way out of this seemingly hopeless situation.

"The queen will see you now," said one of the guards gesturing for Vedavalli to follow him.

"I apologize for the actions of my guards," Queen Meenakshi said, her voice soft. "They were acting on false information, and I take full responsibility for their mistake."

Vedavalli was angry, it took a while for her to display a polite emotion. Vedavalli nodded, her eyes meeting the queen. "I accept your apology," she said.

The queen's smile was as small as a seed, barely perceptible to the naked eye. "I am glad to hear that," she said. "But I also have a proposition for you."

Vedavalli raised an eyebrow, curious. "What proposition?"

Queen Meenakshi leaned forward, her expression serious. "I have heard of your reputation as a skilled investigator and advisor," she said. "And I believe that Anga could benefit from your expertise."

Vedavalli had initially considered the new queen as her prime suspect in the attempted murder of Crown Prince Rajesh. The queen of Anga had both the means and motive to carry out such a heinous act, and her position of power only added to the suspicion. However, the queen's request for help from Vedavalli in solving the crime made the situation more complex; a tangled web, each strand connected to the next, making it difficult to discern the truth.

"I still do not believe that you willingly allowed the guards to seize you. Is Prince Mukund really dead?"

Vedavalli took a deep breath, trying to calm her nerves. She noticed a faint scent of roses in the air, adding a touch of sweetness to the otherwise tense atmosphere. She wondered if the queen had deliberately chosen that fragrance to put her at ease.

"Yes, it is true," Vedavalli replied, her voice steady. "His beloved, Avanti, confirmed it."

As soon as the words left her mouth, Vedavalli realized that she may have given away more information than she intended. She felt a pang of regret, like a stone sinking to the bottom of a river. But if the queen was truly the suspect, she would have already known about Avanti's involvement. It would also give Vedavalli a glimpse into the queen's level of knowledge about Prince Mukund's life and relationships.

The queen's expression remained unreadable. Vedavalli couldn't tell if she was satisfied with her answer or if she was becoming more suspicious.

Her saree was a rich shade of burgundy, embroidered with intricate gold designs that glimmered in the light. The fabric draped elegantly around her, accentuating her regal bearing.

As the guards left, their footsteps fading into the distance, the queen's gaze shifted back to Vedavalli.

"You suspect me, don't you? For trying to kill Crown Prince Rajesh?"

Vedavalli was surprised by her bluntness.

"I have to consider all possibilities," Vedavalli said, her tone measured. "And as the new queen of Anga, you do have the motive and means to carry out such an act."

The queen's expression remained stoic. But Vedavalli could see a hint of anger simmering beneath the surface, like a pot about to boil over.

"I assure you, I had nothing to do with the death of Crown Prince Rajesh," the queen said, her voice laced with icy determination. "And I will do everything in my power to find the culprit and bring them to justice."

"I would not have revealed this but I have to do to win your trust," the queen said defeatedly.

"I put the necklace in your belongings," she confessed. "I wanted to find a way to meet with you without making it look like an official meeting."

Like a boat lost at sea, adrift in a stormy political swell Vedavalli floated, with no land in sight, nowhere to flee. The weight of her responsibility was heavy to bear.

She had suspected the queen of Anga to be the culprit behind Prince Mukund's plight, but now, she was unsure. Vedavalli had spent years honing her investigative skills, but even she was fallible at times.

Her thoughts drifted to her father's condescending looks when she told him about her desire to become an investigator. He had scoffed at her dreams, dismissing them as frivolous and unworthy of a woman of her stature.

Vedavalli felt a twinge of sadness and frustration at the memory. She had always taken her feminity as baggage as if it was her weakness. Her father had wanted her to marry a wealthy and influential man, someone who would help advance their family's status in society. But Vedavalli had always wanted more than a life of comfort and luxury.

She had taken up the role of a bodyguard and investigator, putting herself in danger to protect those who were vulnerable. She had never once questioned her decision, but now, in a strange new land, with Prince Mukund's life hanging in the balance, she was beginning to doubt herself.

Vedavalli took a deep breath, trying to steady her racing thoughts. She reminded herself that she had a job to do, and she had promised to protect Prince Mukund at all costs. She needed to focus on the evidence at hand, rather than her insecurities.

"I see," Vedavalli said, her voice calm and measured. "And why did you feel the need to meet with me in secret?"

The queen's face softened, and Vedavalli noticed a hint of vulnerability in her eyes. "I need your help," the queen said. "There are forces at work in Anga that I do not fully understand. I fear for the safety of my people, and I believe that you are the only one who can help me uncover the truth."

"Why do you not want the king to know?"

The queen's gaze turned contemplative as she spoke. "You know, Vedavalli," she paused, waiting for Vedavalli to approve her use of her first name. "I have always believed that women would make the best comrades in arms."

She paused a hint of sadness in her voice. "We often need to use our strength in more subtle ways, to fight battles that go unseen and unappreciated. Our power lies in our resilience, our ability to endure and overcome the obstacles that are placed in our paths."

"You think the king is involved," Vedavalli continued, the conversation turning more violent than two swords clashing in a fierce battle. It was a daring accusation for an outsider to make, but given that the queen was using Vedavalli as a weapon to thwart her enemies, she hoped to elicit a response without being thrown back into the dungeon like a discarded pawn on a chessboard. The Queen did not answer. Vedavalli took her leave and promised to inform the Queen of any progress.

The queen of Anga was looking at new silks brought in by the traders. She had just sent off the advisor from Malla, and she was still frustrated by the fact that she had been unable to get any useful information from her.

The traders stood by the side, letting the royal tailor feel the clothing. The queen ran her eyes through the collection.

"This is good," she said pointing to the one in the middle.

Just then the king of Anga walked in, and the queen turned to him with a smile.

Dressed in regal attire of crimson and gold, his attire was embroidered with intricate designs and adorned with precious stones. However, his lips were pressed tightly together as if he was struggling to contain his emotions. There was no mistaking it - this was a complicated man, a man who had done things in his past that he was not proud of.

"Did you send her off, the advisor from Malla?"

The queen looked up from the silks and met her husband's gaze.

"I did," she replied, her tone neutral. "She had nothing new to offer us."

"I see," he said quietly. "And what about our advisors? Have they come up with any solutions to our problems with the border?"

The queen sighed. "They've been working hard, but so far, they haven't been able to find a way out of this mess."

The king nodded slowly, his eyes flickering over to the pile of silks on the table.

CHAPTER SIXTEEN

"They want me dead," Avanti said, her voice trembling. "I know too much, and they want to silence me."She could feel the cold sweat running down her back, soaking her clothes. She couldn't stop shivering despite the heat of the night.

Keshav's face remained impassive, but Avanti could see the muscles in his jaw tighten, a sign that he had already suspected what she was about to confess.

Avanti hesitated for a moment, then blurted out the truth. "I think I know why Prince Mukund was framed for the death of our Crown Prince," she said, her voice barely above a whisper.

"The person who hired you? Who was it?" Avanti asked, trying to keep her voice steady.

Keshav frowned, his eyes darkening with a mixture of anger and sadness. "I'm not sure," he said slowly. "But I have my suspicions. I believe that the person who hired me was onto something big, something that someone didn't want them to know about."

"Is Prince Mukund dead?" Keshav found it difficult to accept that a few attackers sneaking into Malla's palace were able to kill him so easily.

Avanti nodded tears flowing down. "I saw the blood with my own eyes."

"You owe it to him, we owe him the truth," he said, his voice sure now, a beacon of hope cutting through the darkness of uncertainty.

Avanti nodded, wiping away her tears with the back of her hand. "I know. And I want to do everything I can to make things right. But how can we prove his innocence when the real culprit is working for the queen?"

Keshav placed a reassuring hand on her shoulder. "We'll figure it out. But right now, we need to focus on keeping you alive."

In the quiet, rustling forests of Anga...

"If the advisor Vedavalli is in Anga, we should seek her help," Avanti said walking as the leaves crunched softly beneath her feet. She walked slowly, her eyes scanning for signs of movement. Now and then, a rustle or a snap would catch her attention, causing her to freeze and listen intently. But the forest was mostly quiet, with only the sounds of nature filling the air.

"You trust her?" Keshav asked skeptically.

"I don't know," Avanti admitted."If she's alone, she'll travel by horseback," Avanti said. "I know where we can intercept her."

"And what if she is not alone?" Keshav asked, voicing Avanti's doubts.

"Then we'll have to be careful," Avanti said. "But I think it's worth the risk. Vedavalli is our best chance at solving this mystery behind the attack."

They had been waiting for hours, and their patience was wearing thin.

As the figure drew closer, Avanti could see that it was indeed Vedavalli. She breathed a sigh of relief and stepped out of the bushes, followed by Keshav.

Avanti rushed over. "Thank goodness we found you," she said, tears welling up in her eyes.

Vedavalli's horse reared up frightened by the ambush and almost threw her down.

Vedavalli quickly regained control of her horse and asked "Who are you?" noticing Keshav first, her hand on the hilt of her sword.

"Advisor," Avanti said, removing the clothing covering her head.

"Avanti?"

Vedavalli exclaimed, surprised to see her here. "Who is this man? Why are you hiding in the middle of the forest"

"This is Keshav," Avanti said quickly before revealing, "We need your help."

Vedavalli sighed, "Let's find a safe place to talk," she said.

Once settling down in a clearing, Avanti took a deep breath and began to speak.

"I think Keshav and I could find out who killed Prince Rajesh."

Vedavalli raised an eyebrow in interest. "Go on," she said, her expression thoughtful.

Keshav spoke up, "We've already gathered some information about the suspects, but we need your help to piece it all together."

Vedavalli leaned forward, her eyes focused on the two of them. "Tell me everything you know," she said.

And so Avanti and Keshav began to narrate the events that had led them to this point, their voices low and urgent as they recounted their findings. Vedavalli listened intently, interrupting occasionally to ask for clarification or to offer her insights.

"I want to help," Vedavalli said finally without revealing her other mission from the Queen of Anga. "But it won't be easy. We'll need to work together, and we'll need to be smart."

Vedavalli could see that Avanti was serious, that she was willing to take risks and make sacrifices to achieve her goals. It was a quality that Vedavalli admired, one that she possessed. But there was something else as well, something that Vedavalli could not quite put her finger on.

"Hide in Kshatriyapuram," she said suddenly, her thoughts racing. "There are always traders moving in and out of the border, that way you will not stand out."

Avanti looked at her quizzically, but Vedavalli did not explain further. Something told her that the death of Prince Rajesh, the attack on Avanti, and the border issue were all somehow connected. She could sense the pieces of the puzzle falling into place, but she could not yet see the bigger picture.

CHAPTER SEVENTEEN

Prince Mukund was treading the palace grounds of Anga for the first time since his quarrel with his uncle, rendering him a trespasser. Everyone in the dimly lit courtroom was fixated on the dance performance, and every eye was glued to the stage. He made a bold leap and landed on the roof of his room with a loud thud. From behind the towering walls adorned with intricate stone sculptures of gods and goddesses, he peered in and out, keeping an eye on the guards' movements. The shadow from the earthen lamp was a dangerous reminder of how easily he could be caught.

Gently gripping the pillar, he descended, flattening himself against the wall, and listened intently as his heart pounded in his chest upon hearing footsteps.

Prince Mukund covered his hands in the cloth pieces he found lying near the diwan. Using this he rifled through the papers, feeling the rough texture of the parchment against his fingertips. He flipped through folders and shuffled through stacks of letters, searching for anything that might incriminate his uncle's wife.

Suddenly, his hand brushed against something cold and metallic. He gasped, his heart racing as he realized what he had found. It was a small key, hidden among the papers.

With trembling hands, Mukund used the key to unlock a hidden drawer in the desk. Inside, he found a small, intricately carved box, adorned with precious gems and delicate gold filigree.

Mukund's ears perked up as the faint sound of anklets reached him from down the hall. The rhythmic jingle grew louder and clearer as the king made his way closer to his chambers. The sound echoed off the walls, filling the air with a soft, melodic chime that seemed to beckon Mukund forward.

As the king entered the room, the jingling sound intensified, filling the space with a sweet, tinkling melody. Mukund pressed himself against the wall, trying to make himself as small and inconspicuous as possible, and held his breath as the king moved about the room.

As the king settled into his desk, Mukund watched from the shadows, waiting for an opportunity to slip away undetected. As the king moved around the room, his eyes fell on Mukund, who had been hiding in the shadows. Mukund froze, his heart racing as he realized that he had been caught.

But instead of calling for the guards, the king simply looked at Mukund with a cold, calculating gaze. "I was expecting you," he said, his voice dripping with malice. "I knew you were alive all along. You ran away like a coward, hoping to escape your punishment. But I never believed for one minute that you were dead."

Mukund felt a surge of anger and fear rise up within him as he faced his uncle. He knew that the king despised him and would do anything to see him punished. But he was determined not to go down without a fight.

"I didn't run away like a coward," Mukund said, his voice shaking with emotion. "I ran away because I knew that you would never believe me. You hate me, and you would do anything to see me suffer."

The tension in the room was palpable as the two men faced each other, their eyes locked in a battle of wills.

Why are the guards not here yet? Mukund thought.

He had expected to be caught and punished, but instead, the king seemed almost amused by his presence.

"Walk away for now, Mukund," the king said with a sly smile. "There is a bigger punishment waiting for you once you know the truth. And trust me, you won't be able to run away from it this time." The king knew something he didn't. He couldn't imagine what kind of punishment could be worse than being accused of murder and forced to flee for his life. But he knew that he couldn't let the king see his fear.

"I'm not afraid of you," Mukund said, trying to sound confident. "Whatever you have planned, I'll face it head-on. I won't run away again."

The king just laughed and shook his head. "Oh, I don't doubt that you'll face it head-on, Mukund. But whether you'll survive it or not is another matter entirely."

While the palace of Anga was shrouded in shadows, Malla was basking in the warmth of the season, with the people going about their daily routines.

"Is she on her way?" Queen Mahadevi asked glancing at the door every few seconds.

"Yes, Your Majesty. It was raining near the border. She should be here by nightfall," Ojayjit responded.

"Good."

Ojayjit did not move, sensing that the Queen wanted to speak further.

"Minister, why do you think I agreed to her plan?" Queen Mahadevi asked, sensing Ojayjit's thoughts.

Ojayjit raised his eyebrows, "I was hoping that this plan will make Prince Mukund leave Malla on his own," she confessed. "This problem is keeping her occupied and distracted."

Ojayjit was surprised at the Queen's selfishness but didn't show any emotion. "Do you think Prince Mukund will stay in Anga once he finds the culprit?" he asked, hoping to gauge the extent to which the Queen was willing to go.

"Maybe. But at least Vedavalli will stop trying to fix others' problems," the Queen replied.

Ojayjit scoffed at the Queen's lack of empathy but quickly regained his composure. "Apologies for the response, Your Majesty," he said, avoiding eye contact.

"Do you have it, Minister Ojayjit?" the Queen asked, referring to the secret job she had given him the day Prince Mukund was attacked.

"Yes, our inspector has accomplished the task," Ojayjit said, handing over the report.

Queen Mahadevi gently smoothed out the creases on the paper. On the top corner was the name in Sanskrit "Vedavalli." She tore it off and put it into the lamp, burning it until it turned to ashes.

Vedavalli raced right to the Queen's quarters after returning to Malla weak and drained.

"I wanted to see you because I had something to share. It was only after much thought that I made this decision."

"Our duty is done," the Queen continued. "The Queen's court will no longer stand by you or your decisions to help Prince Mukund. We have done all that we can, and it is time for us to move on."

Vedavalli was stunned. She couldn't believe what she was hearing. After all the time and effort that they had put in to help Prince Mukund, the Queen was now turning her back on them.

"Very well," she said, her voice low and defeated.

And she was let down by Queen Mahadevi. But who could she turn to? After being humbled by the only person she trusted. She needed help, maybe even an unlikely alliance.

With very little sleep, Vedavalli woke up early the next morning and set out to meet Ojayjit. He will make a deal, one that benefits him. And Vedavalli had the right incentive. She found him in his opulent mansion, surrounded by his many servants and guards. He looked at her with a smug expression on his face, as if he already knew what she wanted.

"Vedavalli, my dear," he said, his voice dripping with condescension. "What brings you to my humble abode?"

"I was hoping we could come to an agreement," Vedavalli said.

Ojayjit raised an eyebrow. "Go on."

"I can offer you something that you want," Vedavalli replied.

"I will give up my seat at the economic development committee in exchange for your help."

Ojayjit leaned back in his chair, considering her words. "And what is the nature of this help that you seek?" he asked.

"Treason," she said finally, the word hanging in the air like a bolt of lightning on a stormy night. The sound of distant thunder rumbled through the walls as if the very heavens were bearing witness to their conversation.

CHAPTER NINETEEN

On the other side of the river outside of Mahendravati, the capital of Malla, there was a forest. Dark and mysterious, one could hear the sound of animals moving in the underbrush. Avanti and Keshav cautiously made their way through the forest, their weapons drawn. With him, Avanti felt different. Keshav listened to anything she had to say and he took her advice.

As they traveled, they encountered several obstacles, including rough terrain and hostile bandits. After a while, they came to a clearing. In the middle of the clearing was a small hut. The hut was made of mud and straw, and it had a thatched roof. There was a fire burning in the hearth, and an old woman was sitting in front of the fire.

The old woman gave Avanti and Keshav food and water, and she let them sleep in her hut.

They introduced themselves as fourth-generation traders of a family that lived in Kshatriyapuram. It was not new. Families in this region were often business-minded and traveled for an extended duration before returning home.

They walked for several hours through the dense forest, with nothing but the sound of their footsteps and the chirping of birds to accompany them.

As they round a bend in the path, a peculiar figure emerges from the shadows, startling them both.

Introducing herself as Anjai, the stranger said that she too is walking towards Kshatiyapuram. She had long, curly hair and was dressed in simple clothes, with a small bag slung over her shoulder. Avanti and Keshav exchanged a look, unsure whether to trust this stranger.

Anjali's smile widened. "I'm going to Kshatriyapuram too! It is my hometown. I've been away for a long time." She paused and looked at Avanti and Keshav. "Do you mind if I join you on the journey?"

Avanti and Keshav exchanged another look, but this time they nodded in agreement. They could use another companion. "Sure, you can come with us," Avanti said.

Keshav spoke before Anjali could ask the question. They have to appear like a normal, happy couple.

"We both are traveling bards. We want to know about Kshatriyapuram's history"

"My father is well-connected in the region, you can find out everything you want to know", Anjali said.

"Appa meet Avanti and Keshav. A newly married couple exploring Malla."

Avanti turned slightly to avoid showing her blushed cheeks. Keshav had suggested they assume the identity of husband and wife while traveling to avoid drawing attention. She wasn't sure how she felt about the idea.

After they had settled down in the heart of the town, Keshav walked up to Anjali's father. "Sir," he said, "This is a very beautiful town. But why is it so chaotic? I saw a few soldiers standing guard at every market road end."

Anjali's father abruptly banged the table with his hands,

"Prince Rajesh came to me. I advised him to bring peace to this beautiful place. He listened. So did the councilwoman Vedavalli."

"But nothing has changed. We still suffer."

Keshav's trigger had worked Anjali's father began talking about how Kshatriyapuram being at the border of Malla and Anga suffered angst from both the kingdoms and that Vedavalli had come for a peace treaty but nothing worked out.

Now they knew that Prince Rajesh supported peace and was even ready to give away the official control of the land to Malla. This could be the motive for whoever wanted Kshatriyapuram to be owned by Anga. This meant that anyone, including the king and queen, could be a suspect. Keshav suspected Prince Mukund, but he couldn't say it in front of Avanti. He had not personally met Prince Mukund, so he couldn't be sure that he couldn't be a suspect.

He must have been staring for way too long into the horizon, Avanti cleared her throat and elbowed him. He came back to the present and said, "Thank you, sir, for hosting us. These are difficult times, but I know that good news will come soon."

"You know what we have to do right?" Avanti put forth a rhetorical question as she stood outside Anjali's house.

"To the durbar of Anga it is then," Keshav said, looking Avanti in the eye. "Are you comfortable going back?"

Avanti broke his gaze and looked down. "Yes," she said softly. She was nervous about going back to Anga, but she knew they had to do it. Keshav wanted to hold her hands, but he held back. He was hiding something from her, and he knew she would hate him once she knew. This was all the time he had with her.

At the break of dawn the next day, they thanked Anjali and her family for their hospitality and then set off.

CHAPTER TWENTY

When Vedavalli arrived at the prayer hall, she saw Queen Mahadevi kneeling in front of the idol. Queen Mahadevi had once told her that she thanked the gods every day for everything, and accepted everything that happened in her life. Vedavalli wondered if Queen Mahadevi would still listen to her and accept her past.

Queen Mahadevi opened her eyes and turned to see Vedavalli standing in the corner, her hands folded in prayer. She turned back to the idol and sprayed it with holy water one last time that day. The guards began closing the doors as the other devotees left one by one.

Vedavalli walked over to Queen Mahadevi, who handed her a small sweet. "My father made me addicted to temple offering," she said. "This is now your responsibility."

Vedavalli tilted her head. "Your Majesty?" she said doubtfully, wondering where this was going to lead.

Queen Mahadevi handed her a report. One corner of the report smelled like burnt parchment. "Whatever anger is in your heart, leave it here at the foot of the gods," she said. "When you exit the temple, you have no past, only future."

Vedavalli's eyes widened as she saw her brother's name and place of birth on the palm leaf manuscript. "If you decide otherwise and continue to pursue your plans, there is no place for you at the council," Queen Mahadevi said, walking away.

Vedavalli stood there for a long time, staring at the report in her hands. So far, she had thought that she had no future, only the past. Can it be any different?

She turned and walked out of the temple, leaving her future and fate at the hands of the gods.

Still shaken over his confrontation with his uncle, Prince Mukund roamed the streets of Anga, dodging crowds and places where he might be recognized. What could the king know that would destroy him? Mukund tried to push those thoughts away, but they kept circling in his mind like a huge spiral. He kept turning, turning down alley after alley, trying to remember where Avanti's house was.

It was after his near-death encounter with his uncle that Mukund decided Avanti should know. It was possible that she could be in danger.

He ducked into an alleyway, trying to clear his head. He was angry, confused, and worried. He leaned against a wall and closed his eyes, trying to think. Picking himself up, he walked to a street vendor selling tea.

"Do you accept 10 panam of gold?" he asked the tea vendor, taking out a couple of gold coins from his shirt. It was good that he managed to sneak out some coins while confronting his uncle.

The tea vendor looked at the coins in Mukund's hand. "Of course," he said. "What would you like?"

Mukund ordered a cup of tea and some sweets. "Thank you," he said, handing the coins to the tea vendor. He took a sip of his tea and looked around the stall. There were a few other people sitting at tables, but no one he recognized.

He turned back to his tea and took another sip. As he was drinking, he glanced out the window and saw a man walking down the street. The man was tall and thin, with a long beard. Mukund didn't recognize him, but there was something about him that seemed familiar. Mukund turned back to his tea, but he couldn't stop thinking about the man. He tried to remember where he had seen him before, but he couldn't place him.

After a few minutes, Mukund finished his tea and stood up to leave. As he was walking out the door, he glanced back at the man on the street. The man was still there, and he was staring right at Mukund.

Mukund stopped in his tracks. He stared at the man for a moment, and then he realized who he was; one of the attackers who had tried to kill him on the night at the palace of Malla. He promised to himself not to forget those faces. He quickly finished his tea and stood up, following the man as he walked away.

The man was dressed in simple clothes, and he looked like just another merchant. But Mukund knew that he was not what he seemed.

The man walked through the marketplace, stopping to talk to people here and there. Mukund followed him, keeping his distance. Finally, the man stopped in front of a stall that was selling spices. He spoke to the stall owner for a few minutes, then turned and walked away. Mukund stopped and stared at the man. The man saw Mukund and his eyes widened in fear. He turned to run, but Mukund was faster. He grabbed the man by the arm and pulled him back.

"What are you doing here?" Mukund demanded.

The man stammered. "I-I'm just a merchant," he said. "I'm here to sell my wares."

"Then why did you run away as soon as you saw me?" Mukund asked.

"Please," he said. "I didn't mean to hurt you. I was just following orders."

"Whose orders?" Mukund asked.

The man hesitated. "I-I don't know her name," he said.

"Her?"

"Yes, someone from the Malla palace."

"What did she want you to do?" Mukund asked.

"She wanted us to scare you," the man said. "She said that if we didn't, she would have our families arrested."

Mukund's heart sank. "Why would she want to scare me?" he asked.

"I don't know," the man said. "But she said we have to keep you alive"

Mukund released the man's arm and let him go. He watched the man scurry away.

Avanti. He recalled with a jolt, he still has to warn her.

He saw the guards standing at the gate of her house, their spears and swords at the ready. They looked like they were expecting trouble. Mukund took a deep breath and walked up to them. Wearing a plain dhoti and his face covered in mud, Mukund looked as far from a jeweled prince as possible.

"I am here to see the Lady of the house. The queen requests her presence," he said, presenting the signet ring he had taken from his chamber to the door guard.

The door guard nodded and scanned Mukund from top to bottom. "The Lady is not available," he said. "She is busy."

"You want me to tell the queen that Lady Avanti is too busy for her?" Mukund asked.

"No, that is not..." The guard stopped himself as one of his companions furiously shook his head, warning him to stop.

Avanti's father opened the door to see the chaos that was happening outside. Avanti's father froze in his spot. "You... You... they said you were dead," he said. "Avanti... Malla... she went back."

Mukund was surprised. "What?"

"I am here to warn you," Mukund said. "Avanti is in danger."

"Guards, take him!" Avanti's father yelled.

CHAPTER TWENTY-ONE

The Queen of Anga, Meenakshi sat in her palanquin, her face hidden. She was on her way to visit a temple in the nearby village. The palanquin was carried by four men, who walked slowly and carefully. The queen's entourage was made up of a dozen guards, who marched ahead of the palanquin and on either side.

As the queen's entourage passed through the streets, people stopped to stare. Prince Mukund followed the throngs of people trying to get a glimpse of the rare sight.

Once out of the capital, the crowd waned and Prince Mukund took this opportunity to jump in front of the palanquin suddenly. The sudden ambush caused the guards to capture him.

The queen then peeked out from behind the veil, curious to see who had dared to interrupt her journey. His sharp features and dark hair were the only things that made him seem like his princely self.

"What do you want?" she asked.

"I want to speak to you," he said. "In private."

The queen hesitated. She didn't trust the prince, but she also was curious as to what made him desperate enough to jump a royal entourage. She nodded, and the guards released him.

"Why are you here? Did the advisor ask you to surrender?" she mocked him.

"Don't tell me you tried to make Vedavalli worship you at your feet," Prince Mukund expelled all pent-up anger. "She would never do that."

"Oh no of course not. She only sees the truth even clearer than you do. I am a greedy woman, yes Prince Mukund. but I did not kill anybody. I simply used the opportunity to do my best as all greedy people do."

Her honesty always took out people for a moment.

"Strangely I want to believe you. If you did not kill Prince Rajesh. Who did?"

The Queen shrugged. "Leave immediately. I will inform the King it was some jilted subject trying to cause terror"

Prince Mukund tilted his head. *What game was she playing?*

He quickly apologized to the soldiers and made way for the entourage to move.

CHAPTER TWENTY-TWO

Vedavalli returned to the house that had abandoned her. She spoke no words to her father, only telling him that she was there on an urgent quest and needed some of her belongings. He directed her to her things, and she started digging through them, trying to find the jewel box in which she had stored the evidence.

She was sensitive to the interests of everyone around her: her father, Prince Mukund, and the queen, even though they had all hurt her. She wanted to give up hope, but she had spent so many years planning for this moment. She had to get justice for her brother, even if it was the only thing she did before she died.

At times, she felt suffocated and wanted to run away as far as she could. She was alone at night, and even after everything she had been through, she still yearned for support and company. She kept walking step by step, as tired as the horse accompanying her journey.

As if on cue, she imagined what her father would say: "Good thing. At least now you will know what happens if you disobey me!" Those sour imaginings didn't do much to improve her morale. She steered her thoughts to how she was going to present her case before the council of Anga.

The royal council of Anga had a smaller ministry, with only seven members unlike Malla having different sub-councils for different portfolios. This meant that the ministers were likely hand-picked by the king and had a close relationship with him.

The carpet in the durbar hall of Anga shined as usual. People stood on both sides, listening to the minister of treasury inform them of major endowments and lending rules. As the minister ended his announcements, people queued to present their grievances.

Vedavalli stood against the wall, trying to hide her face from the whole world. Now standing in line, waiting to address her grievance with the court of Anga. She was a nobody now, someone at the mercy of justice.

She had to prove that her brother was punished unfairly by the king of Anga. She wanted to cry out in frustration, but this was not the time if she has to avenge her brother. The fate that brought Prince Mukund to her is now forcing her to expose her past and reveal herself to the very crowd that caused her pain.

As she walked in a few people recognized her "Isn't she from Malla? Councilwoman"

Vedavalli wanted to laugh at the irony. Now that she was in power, the world was ready to listen to a woman. But she remembered the day when she pleaded to the guards to let go of her brother, and she was met with jeering voices asking her to go bring her father.

Standing in line were Avanti and Keshav. Why are they here?

The Anga kingdom had a strong bureaucracy in place to support the administration. This bureaucracy included ministers, accountants, and other officials who helped the king run the kingdom.

Although the monarch is the most important member of the political body, political thinkers saw the Ministry* or a council of advisers as a significant organ of the state.

One of them asked Vedavalli to come forward and raise the case.

She thought that she would not be able to speak clearly and that she would start crying, but to her surprise, her voice remained even as she said, "My brother was wrongfully accused of a crime he did not commit years ago. He was blamed for stealing Prince Mukund's jewels. Before my father and mother could prove his innocence, the then Chief of Staff, now King of Anga, had him punished with 180 beatings. Unable to bear the pain, my brother passed away from exhaustion. A few of the current council members, are witnesses to this incident."

"Here is the evidence," she said, holding up a manuscript.

The King of Anga's eyes widened. "Could be fake," he said.

The royal scribe was summoned and confirmed that the manuscript leaf material was indeed real.

Vedavalli's heart was pounding as she continued. "The manuscript has the royal emblem that was used by the council members of King Ramachandra."

The crowd gasped. The eldest of the council members stood up to speak. "Who do you suspect, Vedavalli?"

This was the moment she had longed for, the chance to say out loud the name of the one who killed her brother. "It was King Vikrama, the head of the council at that time who gave the order!" she said, and there was a collective gasp. All the councilmen turned towards the throne.

The King of Anga tried to deny it, but the patra* was clear evidence of his guilt. The crowd began to murmur angrily.

"How could you do this?" Vedavalli asked the king. "My brother was innocent! He didn't deserve to die!"

The King's frame shrunk from all these revelations.

"I am sorry," he said finally. "I was wrong to punish your brother."

But it was too late to apologize.

Vedavalli turned to the crowds, her voice loud and clear.

"A ruler who does not feel any sympathy or kindness towards any human, criminal or not, what is to say another injustice won't be committed? I want the King to step down from the throne."

The council looked at each other worrying over the chaos in the court.

CHAPTER TWENTY-THREE

Watching the whole turmoil, Avanti nudged Keshav as if to signal that this is the right time. Keshav stepped forward.

"I am Keshav, a civilian of Anga, I was employed by a mysterious employer who died. We have come to present evidence behind the murder of Prince Rajesh," Keshav jumped to the center to focus all attention on him.

Surprisingly, it was Queen Meenakshi who responded, "Approach the council, young man," she said with no hint of dismay.

Taking a deep breath he reached into his bag. He walked towards the Queen with the box he had kept from the first time he and Avanti found it.

"This is the shard from the ornament that pierced Prince Rajesh's heart. It belongs to a cabinet in the royal quarters."

Avanti looked betrayed. She didn't believe Keshav had figured the person behind all this and he kept it from him.

"The box belonged to the person who employed me. She found it at the scene of Prince Rajesh's murder."

"And how do you know this?" the King remarked angrily.

"Because I employed him" and this time Keshav was taken aback. It was Queen Meenakshi who spoke.

Queen Meenakshi took the cloth covering the shard and examined it. Her eyes widened in the realization of whose room it came from.

"This carving is from the cabinet made for you", she turned to the King.

"You killed your own son?" she turned to the King. Queen Meenakshi recoiled away from him, her eyes wide with horror and disgust. Her mouth was open in shock, and her body trembled.

"You are a monster. I never want to see you again."

The council was looking at him in distaste.

Avanti looked at Keshav, her eyes filled with tears. "Why didn't you tell me?" she asked.

Keshav sighed. "I was afraid," he said. "I didn't want you to hate me."

Avanti shook her head. "I ...You did what you thought was right."

"And you blamed the innocent Prince Mukund for it. He had to run away from the kingdom because of you," she cried at the King.

The council was taken aback by Avanti's outburst. The King's face twisted with betrayal and anger. His eyes narrowed, and his lips pressed together in a thin line. His body tensed, and he stood with his shoulders back and his fists clenched.

Cornered and forced to confront the truth," I was angry with Prince Rajesh for disobeying me. I grabbed him and pushed him. He fell and hit his head on the cabinet. That foolish boy... All his notion of nobility, righteousness". Tears rolled down the King's face.

"My son..., my boy!" he wailed in agony.

"I didn't mean to kill him. The doctor said his internal organs were failing. No choice...."

The eldest of the council cleared his throat.

"The adherence to the rule of law is the fundamental reason for the success of the land of Anga. I hereby propose to remove King Vikrama from power for the injustice committed to the civilian of Malla" his voice paused as turned to face the King

"And for causing the death of Prince Rajesh".

The King of Anga who was standing all along, approached Vedavalli. He got on his knees.

Vedavalli didn't even look him in the eye. He didn't deserve it.

She had wasted years of her life, planning, and agonizing, and here he was on his knees within moments of knowing the truth.

How can it be so easy?

Prince Mukund emerged from the crowd.

The audience gasped. Avanti froze in her spot. Everybody had lied to her.

He went to Vedavalli first, "I am sorry Vedavalli. I did not know such wounds occupied your heart." And then addressed the council.

"I am guilty of hiding myself for long and allowing the rumors of my death to spread. I did it to find out the truth after being attacked multiple times. You can punish me as you see fit" and with that, he knelt in front of the council.

CHAPTER TWENTY-FOUR

Once the dust settled, the new King of Anga was appointed with little resistance. Queen Meenakshi decided to stay in the palace and advise King Mukund. Avanti returned to her father's house, and although he was displeased with her, he allowed her to enter. She was now setting things right, resolving matters with Keshav.

"I feel betrayed. I thought I will not be hurt, but I was heartbroken," Avanti said to Keshav who was begging her to listen to him once.

"I thought we could be friends. Turns out I was wrong."

"Just hear me out once. Please!" he said, with hands clasped together in front of the chest.

But Avanti shook her head. "I can't," she said. "I need to be alone."

Avanti walked for a long time until she came to a quiet spot by the river. She sat down on a rock and stared out at the water. She felt lost and alone.

It was difficult to forget what Keshav had done, but she also knew that she couldn't let it consume her. She had to move on. She had to find a way to heal.

"Vedavalli" she approached the councilwoman, who was seated near the riverbank staring at a faraway boat. Avanti sat down next to Vedavalli, not consoling or offering any sweet words. She just sat there as a silent company.

She sat there for a while until the sun started to set. Then she stood up and started walking back to her home. As she walked, she thought about what had happened. She realized that she needed time to heal. She needed time to process everything that had happened.

As the king of Anga, Mukund was on his way to address the people. Vedavalli waited to catch one last glimpse of him and as prompted he arrived.

She stood in the corner hoping to get a chance to talk to him.

Mukund spotted her, they remained staring at each other not moving even an eyelid. As always, she took it upon herself to address the elephant.

"I am sorry for everything," she said. "You must know that our friendship was genuine, and I acted with your best interests at heart."

Mukund listened, his expression unreadable.

"I indeed sent the mercenaries against you that day at the palace," she continued. "I only told them to hurt you. But once I got to know you, I realized how much of a mistake that was."

Mukund still didn't say anything.

"Goodbye, King of Anga," Vedavalli said. She got on one knee and paid her respects as a former councilwoman, then turned to leave.

She did not even look back once to check if he was looking at her too. She did not have the courage. It was a goodbye, maybe not the last time they would meet.

www.ingramcontent.com/pod-product-compliance
Lightning Source LLC
Chambersburg PA
CBHW022035150726
47990CB00002B/966